For Danielle,
Happy 3rd
Birthday! We
Love you very,
very much!
Al + Kathy

VIKING KESTREL

Viking Penguin Inc., 40 West 23rd Street, New York, New York 10010, U.S.A.
Penguin Books Canada Limited, 2801 John Street, Markham, Ontario, Canada L3R 1B4

Original Swedish-language edition, with illustrations by Ilon Wikland,
published under the title *Draken med de Röda Ögonen* by Raben & Sjogren Bokforlag, Stockholm, 1985

This English translation first published in Great Britain by Methuen Children's Books Limited 1986
First published in the United States of America by Viking Penguin Inc. 1987

Copyright © Astrid Lindgren, 1985
Illustrations copyright © Ilon Wikland, 1985
English translation copyright © Patricia Crampton, 1986
All rights reserved

Printed in Italy
1 2 3 4 5 91 90 89 88 87
Library of Congress catalog card number: 86-50977
ISBN 0-670-81620-5

ASTRID LINDGREN

THE DRAGON WITH RED EYES

Illustrated by Ilon Wikland

Translated by Patricia Crampton

Viking Kestrel

I REMEMBER OUR DRAGON.
I shall never forget that morning in April
when I saw him for the first time. My brother and I
went out to the pigsty to look at the piglets that had
been born in the night. There lay the big mother sow,
with ten piglets jostling each other in the straw.
But all by itself in a corner stood a little green baby dragon,
with angry eyes.

   "What's that?" said my brother, so surprised
that he could hardly speak.

   "I think it's a dragon," I said. "The sow's had ten piglets
and a dragon!"

It was true, though I suppose no one will ever
discover how it happened. I think the sow was as
surprised as we were. She was not particularly fond of her
dragon baby, but she got used to him in time – except
for his biting her every time she fed him, that is.
She disliked it so much that she finally refused
to feed him at all.

So every day my brother and I had to go to the pigsty with food for the dragon, taking small candle-ends, string and corks – the kind of things dragons usually like. The dragon would certainly have starved to death if my brother and I had not kept going to the pigsty with our little basket. All the piglets would grunt hungrily when we opened the pigsty door, but the dragon just stood there, quite still, staring at us with his red eyes. Not a sound did he make until he had finished, when he would belch quite loudly and produce a contented swishing noise by flicking his tail to and fro.

If one of the piglets tried to get any
of his titbits, the indignant dragon
would bite him severely. He really was
a very naughty little dragon.

But we liked him. We would scratch his back
and he seemed to like that. His eyes would glow
bright red with happiness and he would stand
quite still and let himself be scratched.

Once, I remember, he landed in the trough where the sow ate her swill. I can't remember now how he came to fall in, but I shall never forget his expression as he swam about in the swill, quite calm and sure of himself and delighted to find that he could swim.

My brother fished him out with a stick and put him
in the straw to dry. He shook himself,
spraying the swill around him,
and afterwards he laughed his
silent laugh and stared
at us with his red eyes.

Sometimes he might sulk for days, and no one knew why. He would pretend not to hear when we called him, and would stand in a corner chewing straw and generally behaving in a very odd way. My brother and I would get extremely angry with him and decide not to feed him any more.

"Do you hear, you pig-headed thing!" my brother told him on one occasion. "You'll never get so much as another candle-end, so ha–ha!"

But would you believe it – the little dragon began
to cry! Bright tears trickled from his eyes and we
felt so sorry for him.

"Don't cry," I said hastily. "We didn't mean
it, you shall have as many Christmas-tree candles
as you can eat."

Then the little dragon stopped crying
and laughed silently to himself,
flicking his tail to and fro.

On the second of October every year I think of my childhood dragon. For it was on the second of October that he disappeared. The sunset lit up the sky, on that October day so many years ago, making it shimmer with marvellous colours. A haze hung over the meadows. It was one of those evenings filled with longing – though for what, you cannot tell. The little dragon, the sow and all the piglets had been let out into the field for exercise and my brother and I were watching them.

We shivered in the evening air, now chill with mist, and jumped up and down to keep warm. I was thinking that I would soon be off to my warm bed and that I would probably read a story before going to sleep.

Just then the little dragon came up to me. He laid his cold paw against my cheek and his red eyes were full of tears.

And then – oh, it was so strange – then he flew away. We did not know he could fly, but he lifted himself into the air and flew straight into the sunset. In the end we saw him as no more than a tiny black speck against the fiery sun. And we heard him singing. He sang in a perfectly clear little voice as he flew. I believe he was happy.

But I did not read a story that night.
I lay under my quilt and cried
for our green dragon with the red eyes.